TRIASSIC 225,000,000 years ago	Some reptil the sea (ich	
PERMIAN 280,000,000 years ago	Abundance of fish, some early forms of those seen today	Reptiles develop, giving rise to the dinosaurs
CARBONIFEROUS 345,000,000 years ago	Amphibians leave swamps and shallow seas, giving rise to reptiles	Insects, some of huge size. Early reptiles
DEVONIAN 395,000,000 years ago	Great age of fish, giving rise to amphibians	Some fish adapt to life on land. Amphibians
SILURIAN 435,000,000 years ago	Sea scorpions, some reaching a length of 2.5 metres	Small sea scorpions begin to live on land
ORDOVICIAN 500,000,000 years ago	Jellyfish, trilobites and first vertebrates	None
CAMBRIAN 570,000,000 years ago	Trilobites	None
PRE-CAMBRIAN	Life begins with single celled organisms	None

Oligocene   Pleistocene

The study of animals is called Zoology, *and it is one of the most absorbing subjects in the world. There are about one million different kinds of animals on earth — some very large, and some so small you will need a microscope to see them — and every one has its own interesting points.*

Acknowledgments

The authors and publishers wish to acknowledge the following additional illustrative material as follows:
title page and pages 10, 30, 42, 45 (left), 46, photographs by Tim Clark; pages 24, 25, 26, 34 (top), 35 (top), photographs by Natural History Photographic Agency; pages 9, 20, 22, Oxford Scientific Films; pages 50-51, drawings by David Palmer; pages 4, 16, 41, 44, 45 (right), photographs by John Paull; page 38, photograph by H Stanton; pages 13, 34 (bottom), 35 (bottom), 36-37, photographs by M M Whitehead. The title page photograph was taken with the assistance of Loughborough Pet Centre, and the photograph on page 10 with the kind co-operation of International Stores Ltd, Loughborough.

First edition

© LADYBIRD BOOKS LTD MCMLXXXIII

An introduction to
Zoology

by JOHN and DOROTHY PAULL
illustrated by DRURY LANE STUDIOS

Ladybird Books Loughborough

People of all ages enjoy walking in the countryside. During the spring, summer and autumn months, enthusiasts armed with notebooks and cameras tramp through parks and woodland looking for wildlife. Many are naturalists, members of clubs and societies, following a great English tradition. Famous scientists like Charles Darwin and Gilbert White were naturalists who spent their whole lives studying plants and animals.

Hundreds of thousands of different plants and animals share the world with us, and you don't need to wander far to find them. A few minutes' search in the garden can bring you face to face with a myriad of small creatures. There are over one and a quarter million different forms of life, with more probably as yet not discovered. About one million are animals – some huge and others so small you need a microscope to see them.

Charles Darwin

4

Living things are called *organisms*. Organisms are divided into two kingdoms, the kingdom of plants and the kingdom of animals. This book is about the animal kingdom. People who study animals are called *Zoologists* because Zoology is the study of animals. Zoologists are interested in how animals live and how similar animals can be put in a particular group.

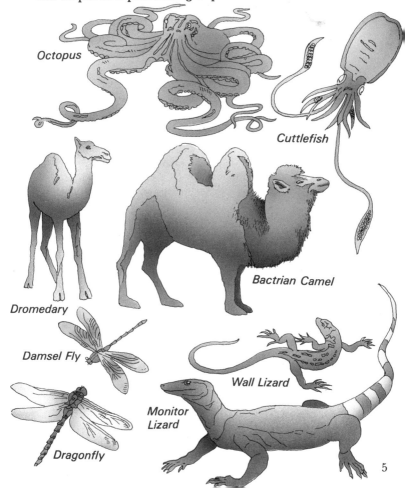

Octopus

Cuttlefish

Bactrian Camel

Dromedary

Damsel Fly

Wall Lizard

Monitor Lizard

Dragonfly

What is a living thing?

To stay alive and keep healthy, all organisms carry out certain life-activities. They breathe, feed, grow, move, reproduce and have young, excrete body wastes, and respond to the environment that surrounds them.

Animals breathe in oxygen from the air and this joins the digested food inside the body, releasing energy which is needed for moving and growing. Breathing and feeding produce waste substances (carbon dioxide, water, mineral salts, and some unwanted food) and as they are not needed they are expelled from the body.

Some creatures have a short life span, such as the mayfly which lives only for a few hours as an adult. On the other hand, an elephant can live for up to seventy years, and a whale as long as ninety years. As they do not live for ever, animals need to reproduce themselves to carry on the species

Animals move in a variety of ways. Some aquatic creatures have thousands of hair-like projections which they use like oars to propel them through the water. Snails use special body muscles to slither along the ground, spiders scuttle on springy legs, and fish glide forward at the swish of a tail.

Most creatures run and hide from danger, often warned by their sense organs. We have five well-developed sense organs that we use to see, touch, smell, hear and taste things around us.

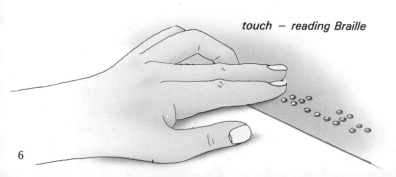

touch – reading Braille

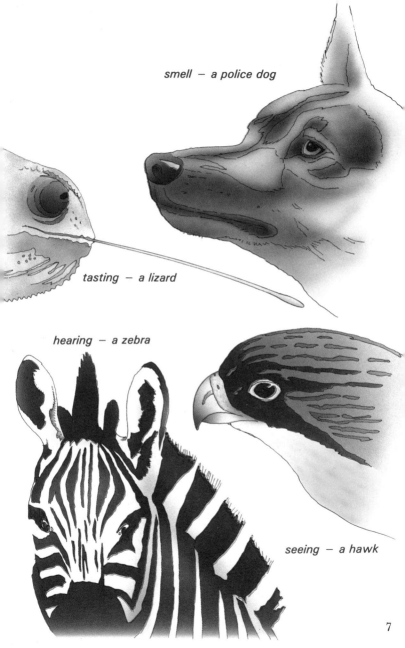

smell — a police dog

tasting — a lizard

hearing — a zebra

seeing — a hawk

7

Cells

All organisms, whatever their shape and size, are composed of *cells*. Cells are so small they can only be seen with a microscope.

The word 'cell' was first used by an Englishman, Robert Hooke (1635-1703), in 1667, when he cut slivers of plant stems and looked at them through a microscope. If you have a microscope, put some onion skin on a slide and look at it through the lens. You will see the individual cells with a low-powered lens. Anton van Leeuwenhoek (1632-1723) built his own microscope, and was the first man to look at animal cells on a microscope slide.

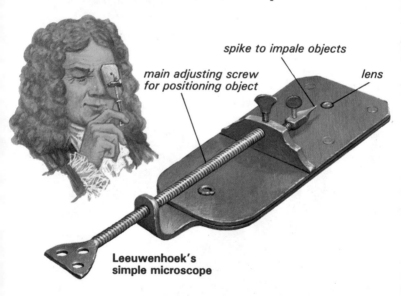

spike to impale objects

main adjusting screw
for positioning object

lens

**Leeuwenhoek's
simple microscope**

Cells are surrounded by a membrane. Inside there is a jelly-like substance called *cytoplasm* and a *nucleus* which controls the living processes of the cells. Membrane, nucleus and cytoplasm together make up *protoplasm*, which is the basis of all living things.

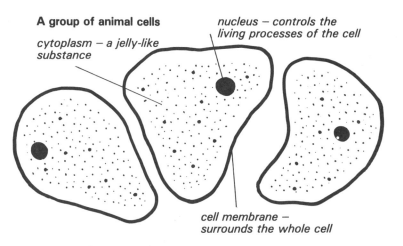

A group of animal cells

nucleus – controls the living processes of the cell

cytoplasm – a jelly-like substance

cell membrane – surrounds the whole cell

onion skin showing cells

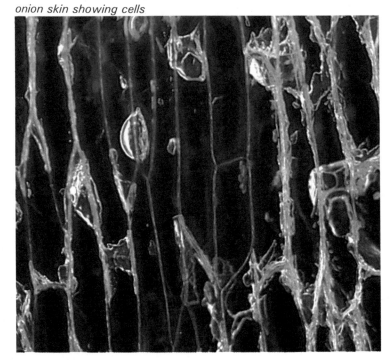

The Classification of Living Things

When you go into a supermarket shopping for, say, a bag of sugar, you look for the sign that reads 'sugar'. The shop staff put the food and other things they sell in groups, such as cereals, soups, bread, frozen food and fish, so that customers can easily find what they need. The food is *classified* into similar groups.

Living organisms may differ in colour, shape and size but they all carry out certain life-activities. A lump of iron does not have any life-activities. It is non-living.

Look at this assortment of things. Can you see the living and non-living things? You are *classifying* the objects into two groups.

Classifying animals

Man probably first classified things according to their usefulness as food. Aristotle (384-322 BC) divided organisms into plants and animals, and subdivided animals according to whether they lived on land, sea or in the air. Later, John Ray (1627-1705) thought that all living things should be given a name, and during his lifetime named over eighteen thousand types of plants.

Today's system of classification comes from Linnaeus (1707-1778).

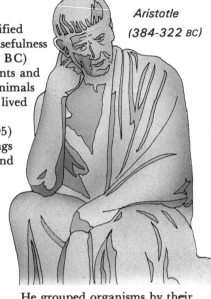

Aristotle (384-322 BC)

He grouped organisms by their body similarities. He decided to name everything in Latin so that the names would be understood by scientists throughout the world. He divided all life into kingdoms, plants and animals, and gave every creature and plant two names. For example, he named the common frog RANA temporaria. Rana is the Latin word for frog, and temporaria means temperate. As the frog lives in cool temperate areas of the world, this description fitted the frog.

Carolus Linnaeus (1707-1778)

To build up a family tree of animals, closely-related *species* are put into a *genus*, similar genera into *families*, families into *orders*, orders into *classes*, and classes into *phyla*.

This is how the frog is classified:

Phylum	Chordata
Sub-Phylum	Vertebrata
Class	Amphibia
Order	Anura
Family	Ranidae
Genus	Rana
Species	Rana temporaria

Invertebrates

The huge animal kingdom is divided into two sections, the single-celled or *unicellular* animals and the many-celled or *multicellular* animals.

Animals without a backbone are called *invertebrates*. All unicellular animals are like this, and so are many multicellular animals. There are many kinds of invertebrates found in most parts of the world and in most types of environments.

Snail

Scorpion

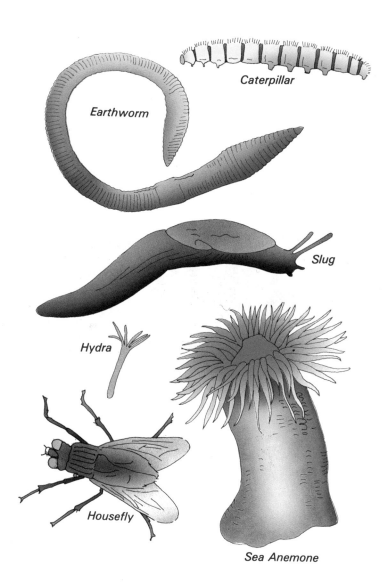

Caterpillar

Earthworm

Slug

Hydra

Housefly

Sea Anemone

15

Protozoa

Fresh water ponds teem with single-celled animals. If there is a pond near your home, try sweeping the water with a net (be sure to choose a safe place to stand) and empty the contents into a white plastic dish. When the water settles, you will be surprised at the number of small creatures swimming in the muddy water.

There are many other forms of water life that you cannot see without a lens or a microscope. A lens that magnifies five times is very useful. Tie it on a cord and hang it around your neck. Can you see any tiny creatures creeping through the slime? If you put a drop of the pond water under a low-powered microscope, you may spot a *protozoan* (a name which means 'first animal') called *amoeba*.

The Amoeba

The amoeba is one of the simplest forms of life. It lives in huge numbers in the slime and mud of ponds and canals. Its name comes from the Greek, *amoibe*, which means 'change'. The amoeba does not have a fixed shape but changes like a blob of treacle, and it is almost transparent.

Inside the single-celled animal is a round nucleus which controls the living functions such as feeding and reproducing, and one or two food vacuoles (which look

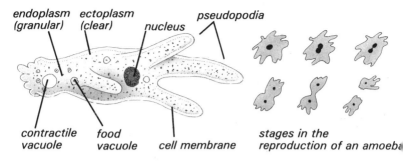

endoplasm ectoplasm nucleus pseudopodia
(granular) (clear)

contractile food cell membrane
vacuole vacuole

stages in the
reproduction of an amoeba

like bubbles) surrounding particles of food. The tiny
creature moves in a streaming motion by pushing out
lobes of cytoplasm called *pseudopodia* (this means 'false
feet'). The amoeba is attracted to food such as minute
plants called *diatoms*, and surrounds them with its
pseudopodia. The plants are slowly digested and the
remains left behind as the amoeba moves along.

The amoeba absorbs oxygen from the water through its
body surface. Waste gases, such as carbon dioxide, pass
from the inside of the animal to the surrounding water.

As the microscopic diatoms are digested in the food
vacuoles, the amoeba uses some of the digested food to
form new protoplasm, and the creature increases in size.
When it reaches a half to one millimetre, the amoeba
splits into two parts. You will also see, in this group of
creatures, *contractile vacuoles,* which pump out excess
water to prevent the animal from bursting. The nucleus
lengthens and divides, the cytoplasm squeezes into a
dumb-bell shape, and eventually the amoeba forms two
new separate creatures.

In hot, dry summers some ponds dry up. If this
happens the amoeba does not die. It draws in its
pseudopodia and forms a hard cyst around itself. When it
rains again and the pond fills, the cyst splits open and the
amoeba resumes its life again, wandering through the
mud looking for food. Sometimes the cell divides in the
cyst stage and new amoebae develop.

17

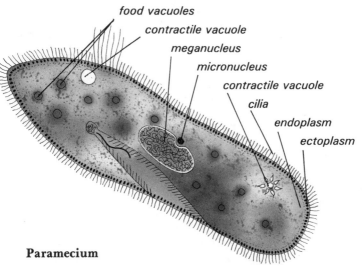

food vacuoles
contractile vacuole
meganucleus
micronucleus
contractile vacuole
cilia
endoplasm
ectoplasm

Paramecium

Many other protozoa live in pond and canal mud. You might find *paramecium* which, unlike the amoeba, has a definite shape. The minute creature has a front end and a back end, a groove leading to a short gullet that ends in the protoplasm, and two nuclei, each different in shape and size from the other.

Each paramecium is covered with hair-like structures, called *cilia*, that wave back and forth like oars, propelling the creature through the water. Cilia also line the groove and force in microscopic plants and animals from the water into the paramecium's body. The prey are digested in food vacuoles, and the waste is eliminated from an opening in the body surface.

A paramecium can reproduce by splitting into two halves, like the amoeba. Sometimes, when conditions in the pond allow, two paramecia join together in the muddy water and exchange nucleus material. When this activity is finished, the two creatures move away and eventually split into two halves, each like the parents.

The paramecium is sensitive to contact with obstacles in the water, such as plants and stones. The animal avoids them by going backwards for a short distance and then moving forwards again, trying and trying again until it gets around the object.

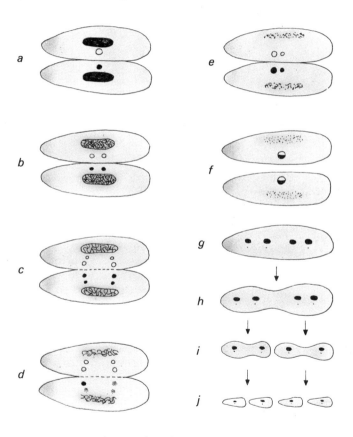

paramecium exchanging nucleus material a − f
and then subdividing g − j

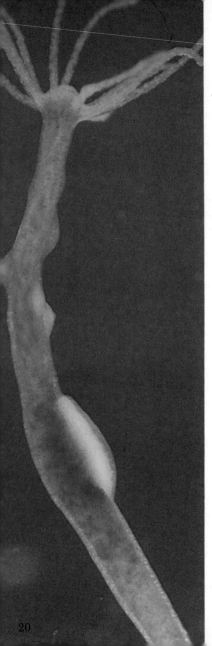

Hydra

The *hydra* is another pond creature. Bigger than the amoeba and the paramecium, the hydra's body contains lots of cells. It is shaped like a cylinder and sticks to plants and rocks, waving thin tentacles in the hope of catching food. The creature grows to about one centimetre, but when it is touched by something in the water, its tentacles withdraw and the hydra curls into a minute green (or brown) blob.

The hydra's body wall has two layers of cells, the outer *ectoderm* and the inner layer called the *endoderm*. There are *stinging cells* with barbed threads on the tentacles. When a small creature touches the tentacles, the stinging cells explode and shoot the barbed threads into the prey. Poisonous fluid paralyses the unfortunate creature, and the tentacles wrap around it and push it into the hydra's mouth. The prey is digested inside the body.

magnified view of hydra, with tentacles extended

Sometimes the hydra moves very slowly by sliding along on its sticky base. It can move faster by 'looping'. Its body bends over until the tentacles touch the surface to which the animal is attached. The sticky foot releases its grip and the hydra swings the base over the tentacles and a fresh grip is made.

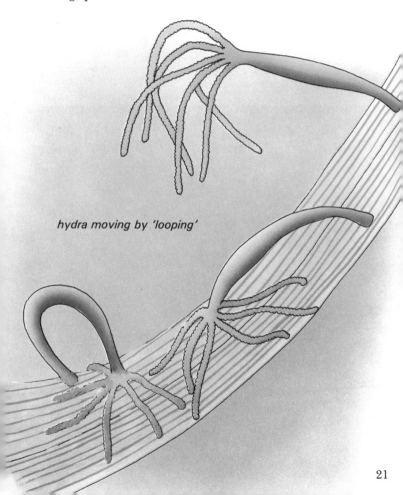

hydra moving by 'looping'

How the hydra reproduces

Sometimes the hydra's tentacles accidentally split from the trunk. When this happens, the hydra grows new tentacles to replace the damaged ones. Also, if the whole body is cut in half, each part develops into a new hydra. This is called *regeneration* and is a characteristic of several kinds of small creatures.

When there is plenty of food available, the hydra reproduces by *budding*. A solid bulge develops half way along the animal's body, and this soon grows tentacles. A sudden squeeze forces the young hydra to 'bud' off and the new creature waves its tentacles, floating through the water until it lands on a plant or rock.

hydra releasing egg or ovum

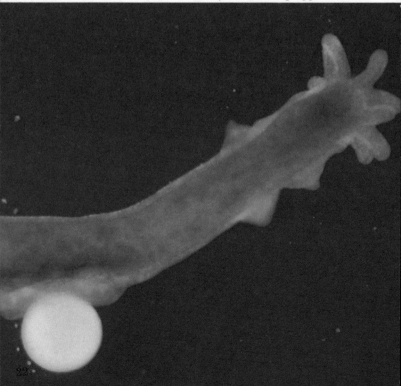

The hydra can also develop male and female body parts which do not ripen at the same time, so that the animal cannot fertilise itself. The *testes*, the male organs, grow under the tentacles, releasing sperm cells which swim to the female organ, the *ovary*, of a nearby hydra. Some time later, the fertilised *ovum* (egg) drops to the bottom of the pond and develops into another hydra, which loops its way to a suitable spot for collecting food.

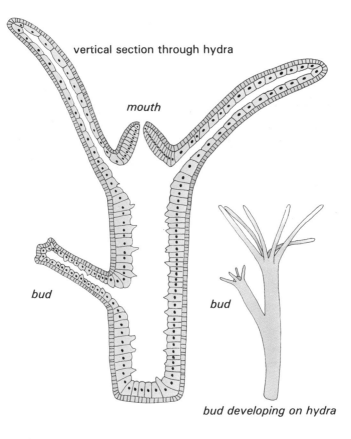

vertical section through hydra

mouth

bud

bud

bud developing on hydra

The earthworm

The earthworm lives in the earth, coming out at night to forage for food. As it moves through the soil, the earthworm forms 'worm casts' on the garden surface — an activity that keeps the earth healthy. Charles Darwin studied the worm and he calculated that about fifty thousand worms live in a medium-sized field, bringing massive amounts of rich soil to the surface each year.

Dig up a worm in your garden, hold it carefully in your hand and look at it with your lens. Can you see the body segments? Each segment has short, stiff bristles which help the creature to move. It has a tiny mouth, but there aren't any eyes or ears. An earthworm can tell when it is near the soil surface because its head is sensitive to light.

When you have looked closely at the earthworm, don't forget to return it to your garden!

Earthworms mating during damp weather

The earthworm is *hermaphrodite*, which means that each worm is male and female, but, like the hydra, needs a partner to reproduce. The exchange of male sperms happens during damp weather. Two worms lie together facing opposite directions and then exchange sex cells. The worms then move away from one another and develop *cocoons*. The rubbery cocoons contain eggs and sperm. The creatures grow a thick circular band of skin, the *saddle*, around the cocoons. Eventually the cocoons are left in the soil, splitting and releasing three or four little worms which wriggle away to begin their life.

Worms are often injured by gardeners. If a worm is sliced in half by a garden spade, the two pieces usually regrow into complete worms.

The housefly

The housefly, like all insects, has three parts to its body: the *head*, the *thorax* and the *abdomen*. Grey in colour and marked with black streaks, the housefly is covered in short bristles. On top of its head there are three simple eyes and two large compound eyes. It also has two antennae and six legs. There are two small claws on each leg and two pads which secrete a sticky substance which helps it to cling to any surface it walks on. It has one pair of wings.

Our gardens and kitchens provide food and shelter to the housefly. The creature is a nuisance and a threat to our health because it forages in smelly, rotting food outside and then is likely to land on food we eat, infecting it with germs.

The female housefly lays batches of eggs from June to September, as many as a hundred and fifty eggs in each batch. In hot weather, the eggs develop quickly and hatch into maggots or larvae in twenty-four hours, but in cooler conditions this may take days, or even a week or two. The full grown maggots are about one centimetre long, white in colour, with a black hooked-shape spine used for tearing food into small pieces and for dragging themselves along. The maggots moult twice and are fully grown after five days. They wriggle to a safe, dry spot and change into pupae, changing colour from white to brown. This process, typical of insects, is called *metamorphosis*. The adult flies crawl out of the pupae in about four days, and the new females begin to lay eggs in two weeks. Thousands of flies develop in the summer months in garden compost. Most of them die at the end of the year, although some manage to hibernate through the winter.

larva

eggs

pupa

adult

Vertebrates

Creatures that have an internal bony skeleton and a backbone are called *vertebrates*. The vertebrates are much less numerous than the invertebrates but are much more familiar to us.

Vertebrates are divided by zoologists into five classes:

PISCES — The animals in this class are cold blooded and breathe through their gills. They are covered by scales and are called *fish*.

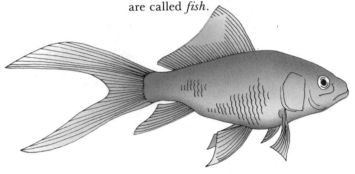

AMPHIBIANS — *Amphibians* are cold blooded and have a soft, moist skin. When they are young they breathe through gills. They develop lungs when they become adult. Frogs, toads and newts are amphibians.

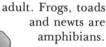

REPTILIA

Reptiles have dry skin covered with hard, overlapping scales. They breathe through lungs. The offspring, which look like their parents, develop from eggs.

AVES   Members of the aves are called *birds*. Birds have fore-limbs developed as wings which are covered with feathers. They have scales on their legs, and, like the reptiles, the young develop from eggs.

MAMMALIA

The skin of a *mammal* is covered with hair. The young develop inside the mother and are fed on milk from *mammary glands*. Typical mammals are dogs, cats, horses, cows, and man.

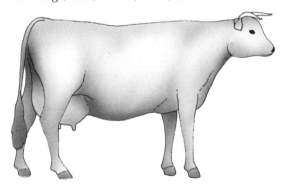

Vertebrates

Class: Pisces

Most fish, such as the herring and the cod, have hard, bony skeletons. Some others, especially members of the shark family, have skeletons made from a softer substance called *cartilage*. Most fish are streamlined so that they can move easily through the water, moving the tail and tail fin from side to side.

If you have a goldfish, look at the gill cover on each side of its head. Beneath these flaps are the gills. Goldfish, like all fish, breathe by gulping water into the mouth and passing it through the gills. Inside the gills the oxygen in the water joins the blood and is pumped around the fish's body. Look at the eyes of your goldfish as it swims around the bowl. They are large and do not have eyelids. The eyes are covered with a transparent skin that protects the eyes from injury. There is a small snout above the mouth which the fish uses for smelling its food.

A goldfish is completely covered with thin overlapping scales and a delicate slimy skin which protects the body from bumps and scrapes. Down the centre of the body runs a line of sensitive cells which feel vibrations in the water.

Some kinds of fish give birth to live young, but most lay eggs and sperm in the water, where fertilisation takes place. The eggs drift until they hatch, but are easy prey for hungry fish. A cod lays five million eggs and the herring up to sixty million a year, but only a small number of these will survive to be adults.

Cod

Herring

Amphibians: The frog

Like toads and newts, the frog is cold blooded, living in and around ponds and slow running streams. Its body is squat and flat, an ideal shape for leaping and swimming, helped also by very strong hind legs and webbed feet. The frog has two large bulging eyes which, when the creature is swimming, often lie just above the water level, giving good all-round vision. It feeds on beetles, flies, spiders and worms, using its long sticky tongue to flick and catch unsuspecting prey. The food is then forced alive into the frog's stomach, where digestion occurs.

eggs or 'frog spawn'

back legs develop

developing tadpoles

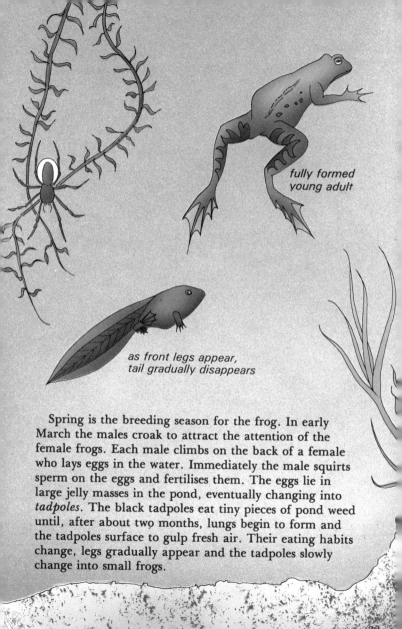

fully formed
young adult

as front legs appear,
tail gradually disappears

Spring is the breeding season for the frog. In early March the males croak to attract the attention of the female frogs. Each male climbs on the back of a female who lays eggs in the water. Immediately the male squirts sperm on the eggs and fertilises them. The eggs lie in large jelly masses in the pond, eventually changing into *tadpoles*. The black tadpoles eat tiny pieces of pond weed until, after about two months, lungs begin to form and the tadpoles surface to gulp fresh air. Their eating habits change, legs gradually appear and the tadpoles slowly change into small frogs.

Reptiles

Crocodiles, tortoises, snakes and lizards are reptiles. They are cold blooded creatures, and have scales or horny plates covering their bodies. Some reptiles produce young alive, whilst others lay soft, rubbery eggs. Lizards and adders give birth to live young. This process is called *viviparity*.

Aldabra Giant Tortoise

Adder

The young develop from an egg inside the mother's body. This method of reproduction is much safer than leaving eggs in a nest or hiding place where they could be taken by predators. Reptiles which lay eggs include the tortoise and the turtle, most snakes, crocodiles and alligators.

Nile Crocodile

Common Lizard

Grass Snake

Grass snakes

Grass snakes are limbless reptiles which live in England and Wales, but not Scotland or Ireland. They have long slender bodies and half-moon shaped markings near the head. Grass snakes can grow to over one metre.

These shy creatures are not poisonous, and spend the summer months basking in the sun on warm rocks, sheltering under rocks when it gets cold and wet. They catch small birds, frogs and lizards for food, swallowing the prey whole. The lower and upper jaws move independently so the mouth opens wide enough to cope with any struggling creature.

Grass snakes' bodies, like all reptiles, are covered with dry scales. The creatures breed when they are about three years old, mating in April or May on warm, sunny days. Eggs are laid usually in June in warm, decaying vegetable matter. The developing young feed off the egg yolk as they grow. Hatching occurs in about two months, and the newly-formed snakes measure about ten centimetres.

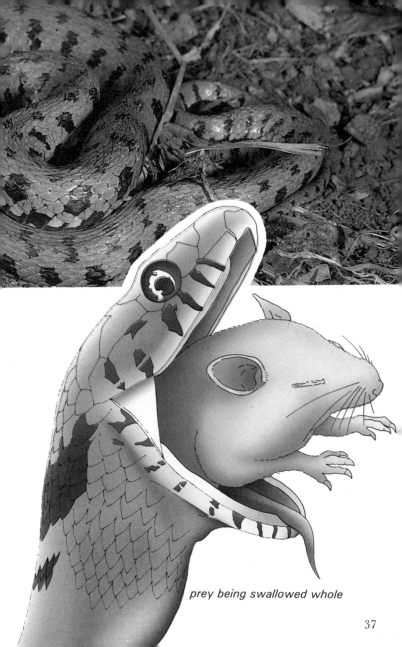

prey being swallowed whole

Aves: Birds

Birds have probably descended from reptiles, because they resemble the reptiles in some ways. It may be that they evolved from small reptilian dinosaurs which hunted by jumping down from trees or rocks. They developed wings so that they could glide — the beginning of flight.

A bird's body has a head, a neck, a trunk and a tail. Usually the body is small, light and streamlined, the ideal shape for flying at speed. The feathers overlap and point backwards so that they are not ruffled by the air during flight. The feathers, like the scales on a reptile, protect the bird from unpleasant weather and keep the skin warm and dry. Any feathers that get broken develop again after

Starling

the bird has moulted. The legs are covered in scales (again, like the reptiles) and there are pointed claws on the toes. Some birds, such as hawks and owls, have long claws: an ideal shape for catching and killing small animals. Others, such as the chicken, have blunt nails for scratching in the earth for seeds and worms. Some water birds have webbed feet.

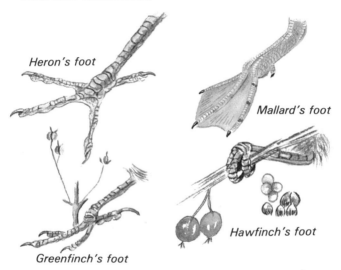

Heron's foot

Mallard's foot

Hawfinch's foot

Greenfinch's foot

The bird's jaw is pointed to form a beak. Ducks have flat beaks which they use for sieving particles of food from the mud in ponds and estuaries.

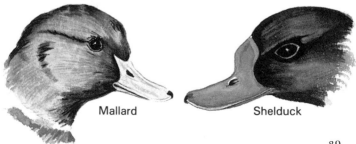

Mallard

Shelduck

Finches have hard, pointed beaks for opening seeds, and herons have long, slender beaks which they use for catching frogs and fish.

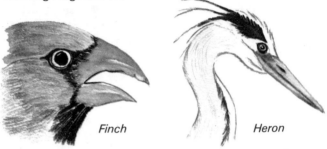

Finch

Heron

Sense organs

A bird has a very keen sense of sight and hearing. Its eyes are large and protected by two eyelids and a thin transparent skin which keeps the eyes clean. The ear opening is behind the eye and there is no external ear lobe.

the keen eye of a bird of prey

Hedgesparrow nest with Cuckoo egg

Reproduction

All birds lay eggs which have hard brittle shells. The eggs are often laid in nests where they are incubated by the parent sitting on them. Young birds are usually cared for by one or both parents during the early stages of development, feeding and tending them until they are ready to fly away and live on their own.

Winter is a hard and tiring period for many birds. Some come into gardens looking for food, and this gives us a good opportunity to study them from our homes. As food is scarce in the countryside, the birds can be attracted to a bird-table if you put out some bread.

Mammals

Mammals evolved over two hundred million years ago. There are many different kinds of mammals, most of which live on land. Their bodies are usually covered in hair, and some mammals, such as cats and dogs, have a thick coat of fur.

Mammals breathe through lungs, even if they live in the sea. Whales come to the surface regularly to breathe gulps of air. Like birds, the mammals are warm blooded, but nearly all of them also have sweat-glands which get rid of excess body heat by producing small amounts of water. Young mammals develop and grow inside their mother, and when born, feed on milk formed in the parent's body.

Cuvier's Beaked Whale
(2 colour phases)

Bottle-nosed Whale

Killer Whale

Sperm Whale

43

Mammals: The cat

The cat is a social animal that lives contentedly in our homes, coming and going much as it pleases. The fur can be a variety of colours. A cat's eyes are one of its distinctive features. For a hunting animal, the eyes are very well placed in a forward-pointing position. When the animal is on the prowl (usually at night), its eyes pick up the slightest movement and the cat uses its ears and nose to detect squeaks and smells. Once spotted, small rodents fall easy victim to the furry hunter. The cat is a natural hunter, killing its prey with sharp claws or a bite in the neck. We often supplement a cat's diet by giving it meals of fresh fish and liver.

Cats give birth between sixty and seventy days after mating. Usually the female gives birth and cleans the new born kittens without any assistance, although sometimes another female may help her. The kitten's eyes are closed at first, and the ears folded down flat. Quickly, like all new born mammals, the unseeing kitten sucks life-giving milk from its mother's mammary glands. After three weeks the kitten is able to see and is strong enough to move around. At eight weeks a full set of sharp teeth appear, and the young animal begins to eat solid food.

Mammals: Man

Man is considered the most highly developed organism of all. Because he has the power to think clearly and reason logically, he is considered superior to other forms of life.

Man's body is a wonderful machine, made up of millions of cells. His head, neck, trunk, arms and legs are held together by muscles and a strong skeleton. The skeleton protects important body organs, such as the brain, heart and lungs.

Like all mammals, Man breathes in air into his lungs and expels carbon dioxide. Some oxygen is removed from the air in the lungs and is absorbed by the blood. Together with digested food, the oxygen nourishes the body cells. Waste carbon dioxide gas from the cells is carried to the lungs by the blood and leaves the body in the air we breathe out.

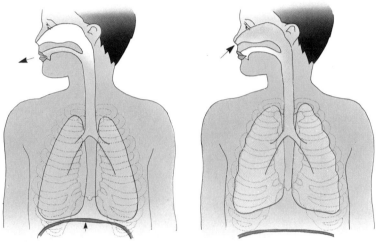

Most animals, including Man, use the *sexual* method of reproducing. This means that individuals of each of the two sexes (male and female), produce material for the new individual. The male produces sperm cells which combine with the egg cells produced by the female parent. The joining together of the egg and the sperm is called fertilisation, and the result is called the *zygote*. The zygote eventually forms an *embryo* from which the new animal develops. When it has matured, the new animal can produce egg or sperm cells, so that it can reproduce like its parents. In this way, each generation produces a new generation and the species continues to exist.

Man

Man's body is active all the time, even when he is asleep. The body functions are controlled by the *brain*, a large organ protected by the skull. When awake, man is aware of the environment around him and his sense organs are continually sending signals to the brain. Sight is perhaps the most important of the five senses because it gives the brain so much information about the surroundings. As the eyes are very delicate, they are protected, and rest in bony sockets in the skull.

In many ways man has control over his environment, and can alter it to suit his needs. Because he is very curious, he has learned a great deal about his fellow creatures and is aware how living things depend on each other.

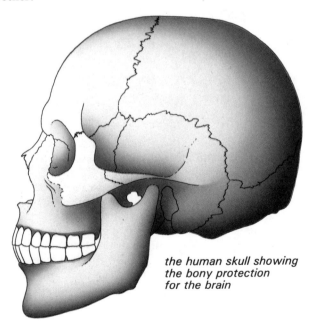

the human skull showing the bony protection for the brain

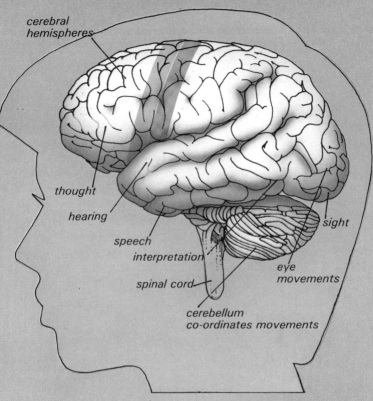

cerebral
hemispheres

thought

hearing

speech

interpretation

spinal cord

sight

eye
movements

cerebellum
co-ordinates movements

Tongue,
lips and jaw control

Face movements

Neck movements

Hand control

Arm control

Body movements

Leg control

*MOTOR AREAS
– send messages
to different parts
of the body*

*SENSORY AREAS
– receive messages
from different parts
of the body*

*the left and right
hemispheres
of the brain
seen from above*

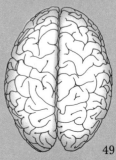

The interdependence of living things

There are hundreds of different animals living in a healthy pond. Fish, frogs, newts, insects, worms and microscopic creatures live together in the water and depend on each other for survival. A pond is a natural community, inhabited by populations of different creatures.

Big fish live on smaller fish. The small fish depend on water plants for food and shelter. Both the fish and the plants would die if the snails and microscopic organisms that live on the bottom were removed. These populations remove dead and decaying materials by eating them.

There are many kinds of natural communities. A field is a community — and so is a hedgerow and a tree.

Heron

Kingfisher

Duck

Pike

two kinds of natural communities
above — woodland
below and left — a pond

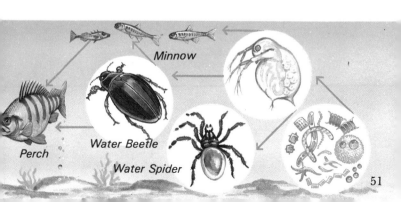

Minnow

Perch

Water Beetle

Water Spider

INDEX

By Iain Gray

Lang**Syne**

PUBLISHING

WRITING *to* REMEMBER

LangSyne

PUBLISHING

WRITING *to* REMEMBER

79 Main Street, Newtongrange,
Midlothian EH22 4NA
Tel: 0131 344 0414   Fax: 0845 075 6085
E-mail: info@lang-syne.co.uk
www.langsyneshop.co.uk

Design by Dorothy Meikle
Printed by Printwell Ltd
© Lang Syne Publishers Ltd 2016

ISBN 978-1-85217-226-8

Forsyth

MOTTO:
A repairer of ruin.

CREST:
A griffin.

TERRITORY:
Fife, Stirling, Lanarkshire.

*Echoes of a far distant past
can still be found in most names*

Chapter one:

Origins of Scottish surnames

by George Forbes

It all began with the Normans.

For it was they who introduced surnames into common usage more than a thousand years ago, initially based on the title of their estates, local villages and chateaux in France to distinguish and identify these landholdings, usually acquired at the point of a bloodstained sword.

Such grand descriptions also helped enhance the prestige of these arrogant warlords and generally glorify their lofty positions high above the humble serfs slaving away below in the pecking order who only had single names, often with Biblical connotations as in Pierre and Jacques.

The only descriptive distinctions among this peasantry concerned their occupations, like Pierre the swineherd or Jacques the ferryman.

The Normans themselves were originally Vikings (or Northmen) who raided, colonised and eventually settled down around the French coastline.

They had sailed up the Seine in their longboats in 900AD under their ferocious leader Rollo and ruled the roost in north east France before sailing over to conquer England, bringing their relatively new tradition of having surnames with them.

It took another hundred years for the Normans to percolate northwards and surnames did not begin to appear in Scotland until the thirteenth century.

These adventurous knights brought an aura of chivalry with them and it was said no damsel of any distinction would marry a man unless he had at least two names.

The family names included that of Scotland's great hero Robert De Brus and his compatriots were warriors from families like the De Morevils, De Umphravils, De Berkelais, De Quincis, De Viponts and De Vaux.

As the knights settled the boundaries of their vast estates, they took territorial names, as in Hamilton, Moray, Crawford, Cunningham, Dunbar, Ross, Wemyss, Dundas, Galloway, Renfrew, Greenhill, Hazelwood, Sandylands and Church-hill.

Other names, though not with any obvious geographical or topographical features, nevertheless derived from ancient parishes like Douglas, Forbes, Dalyell and Guthrie.

Other surnames were coined in connection with occupations, castles or legendary deeds.

Stuart originated in the word steward, a prestigious post which was an integral part of any large medieval household. The same applied to Cooks, Chamberlains, Constables and Porters.

Borders towns and forts – needed in areas like the Debateable Lands which were constantly fought over by feuding local families – had their own distinctive names; and it was often from them that the resident groups took their communal titles, as in the Grahams of Annandale, the Elliots and Armstrongs of the East Marches, the Scotts and Kerrs of Teviotdale and Eskdale.

Even physical attributes crept into surnames, as in Small, Little and More (the latter being 'beg' in Gaelic), Long or Lang, Stark, Stout, Strong or Strang and even Jolly.

Mieklejohns would have had the strength of several men, while Littlejohn was named after the legendary sidekick of Robin Hood.

Colours got into the act with Black, White, Grey, Brown and Green (Red developed into Reid, Ruddy or Ruddiman). Blue was rare and nobody ever wanted to be associated with yellow.

Pompous worthies took the name Wiseman, Goodman and Goodall.

Words intimating the sons of leading figures were soon affiliated into the language as in Johnson, Adamson, Richardson and Thomson, while the Norman equivalent of Fitz (from the French-Latin 'filius' meaning 'son') cropped up in Fitzmaurice and Fitzgerald.

The prefix 'Mac' was 'son of' in Gaelic and clans often originated with occupations – as in

MacNab being sons of the Abbot, MacPherson and MacVicar being sons of the minister and MacIntosh being sons of the chief.

The church's influence could be found in the names Kirk, Clerk, Clarke, Bishop, Friar and Monk. Proctor came from a church official, Singer and Sangster from choristers, Gilchrist and Gillies from Christ's servant, Mitchell, Gilmory and Gilmour from servants of St Michael and Mary, Malcolm from a servant of Columba and Gillespie from a bishop's servant.

The rudimentary medical profession was represented by Barber (a trade which also once included dentistry and surgery) as well as Leech or Leitch.

Businessmen produced Merchants, Mercers, Monypennies, Chapmans, Sellers and Scales, while down at the old village watermill the names that cropped up included Miller, Walker and Fuller.

Other self explanatory trades included Coopers, Brands, Barkers, Tanners, Skinners, Brewsters and Brewers, Tailors, Saddlers, Wrights,

Cartwrights, Smiths, Harpers, Joiners, Sawyers, Masons and Plumbers.

Even the scenery was utilised as in Craig, Moor, Hill, Glen, Wood and Forrest.

Rank, whether high or low, took its place with Laird, Barron, Knight, Tennant, Farmer, Husband, Granger, Grieve, Shepherd, Shearer and Fletcher.

The hunt and the chase supplied Hunter, Falconer, Fowler, Fox, Forrester, Archer and Spearman.

The renowned medieval historian Froissart, who eulogised about the romantic deeds of chivalry (and who condemned Scotland as being a poverty stricken wasteland), once sniffily dismissed the peasantry of his native France as the jacquerie (or the jacques-without-names) but it was these same humble folk who ended up overthrowing the arrogant aristocracy.

In the olden days, only the blueblooded knights of antiquity were entitled to full, proper names, both Christian and surnames, but with the passing of time and a more egalitarian, less feudal atmosphere, more respectful and worthy titles spread throughout the populace as a whole.

Echoes of a far distant past can still be found in most names and they can be borne with pride in commemoration of past generations who fought and toiled in some capacity or other to make our nation what it now is, for good or ill.

Chapter two:

For Scotland's cause

The origin of the name of Forsyth has never been determined with certainty, but at least three possible sources have been identified.

Whatever the origins, however, what is beyond doubt is that bearers of the name have flourished in Scotland since at least the twelfth century.

One tradition holds that the progenitor, or 'name-father' of the Forsyths was one of the wild and sea-roving Norsemen, by the name of Forsach, who eventually settled in present-day France, in the region of Aquitane.

One of his descendants, the Viscomte de Fronsoc, is recorded at the court of England's Henry III between 1236 and 1246.

His family were granted lands in the north of England, and are believed to have later settled in the Scottish Borders.

From here, they gradually spread

throughout Scotland, particularly in Lanarkshire, Stirling, and Fife.

A David Forsyth, who was in possession of lands in the Strathaven area of Lanarkshire as early as the mid to late fifteenth century, proudly and adamantly claimed a descent from the Viscomte de Fronsoc, while the family castle at Dykes dominated the local landscape until it was finally demolished in 1828.

One intriguing mystery concerning the name of Forsyth is that early records designate some bearers as 'de Forsyth' ('of Forsyth'), indicating that the name may have its origins as a territorial or 'location' name.

A Thomas de Forsith is recorded in Glasgow in the latter decades of the fifteenth century, while a William de Fersith is recorded in Edinburgh in the sixteenth century.

No actual 'Forsyth' place name, however, has ever been identified.

Another possible source of the name is from the Scottish Gaelic 'fear sithe', meaning 'man of peace', while some authorities speculate that rather than indicating 'man of peace', the name may indicate 'place of peace'.

It would be rather ironical if the origin of the name is indeed from 'man of peace', or 'place of peace', considering the bloody lives and times of generations of Forsyths who distinguished themselves as brave defenders of Scotland's freedom and independence and doughty defenders of their religious ideals.

A William de Fersith was one of the reluctant signatories in 1296 to a humiliating treaty of fealty to the conquering Edward I of England, who was known as 'the Hammer of the Scots'.

Signed by 1,500 earls, bishops, and burgesses, the parchment is known as the Ragman Roll because of the ribbons that dangle from the seals of the signatories.

This humiliation was avenged in May of the following year, however, when William Wallace raised the banner of revolt against the English occupation of Scotland.

Proving an expert in the tactics of guerrilla warfare, Wallace and his hardened band of freedom fighters inflicted stunning defeats on the English garrisons.

This culminated in the liberation of practically all of Scotland following the battle of Stirling Bridge, on September 11, 1297.

Despite having a force of only thirty-six cavalry and 8000 foot soldiers, compared to an army under the Earl of Surrey that boasted no less than 200 knights and 10,000 foot soldiers, the Scots held a strategic advantage that they exploited to the full.

Positioning their forces on the heights of the Abbey Craig, on the outskirts of Stirling, and where the imposing Wallace Monument now stands, Wallace and his commanders waited patiently as Surrey's force slowly made its way across a narrow wooden bridge that spanned the waters of the Forth.

As the bulk of the English army crossed onto the marshy ground at the foot of the Abbey Craig, the piercing blast of a hunting horn signalled a ferocious charge down the hillside of massed ranks of Scottish spearmen.

Trapped on the boggy ground, the English were incapable of putting up any effective resistance.

They were hacked to death in their hundreds, while many others drowned in the fast-flowing waters of the Forth in their heavy armour as they attempted to make their way back across the narrow bridge.

Defeated at the battle of Falkirk on July 22, 1298, after earlier being appointed Guardian of Scotland, Sir William Wallace was eventually betrayed and captured in August of 1305, and, on August 23, he was brutally executed in London on the orders of a vengeful Edward I.

The beacon of freedom was soon re-ignited under the inspired leadership of Robert the Bruce, however, who was enthroned as King of Scots in an ancient ceremony at Scone Abbey in March of the following year.

One of his earliest supporters appears to have been Osbert Forsyth, because it is only a short time after 1306 that Bruce granted him lands at Sauchie, in Stirlingshire.

Forsyth also fought with distinction at the side of the great warrior king at Bannockburn in June of 1314, when a 20,000-strong English army under Edward II was defeated by a Scots army less than half this strength.

By midsummer of 1313 the mighty fortress of Stirling Castle was occupied by an English garrison under the command of Sir Philip Mowbray.

Bruce's brother, Edward, agreed to a pledge by Mowbray that if the castle was not relieved by battle by midsummer of the following year, then he would surrender.

This made battle inevitable, and by June 23 of 1314 the two armies faced one another at Bannockburn, in sight of the castle.

It was on this day that Bruce slew the English knight Sir Henry de Bohun in single combat, but the battle proper was not fought until the following day, shortly after the rise of the midsummer sun.

The English cavalry launched a desperate but futile charge on the densely packed ranks of

Scottish spearmen known as schiltrons, and by the
time the sun had sank slowly in the west the
English army had been totally routed, with
Edward himself only narrowly managing to make
his escape from the carnage of the battlefield.

Scotland's independence had been
secured, to the glory of Bruce and loyal supporters such as Osbert Forsyth, who was rewarded in
1320 with confirmation of the grant of his lands.

Chapter three:

King and Covenant

The Forsyths were recognised as able administrators in the service of the Crown, with Osbert Forsyth's son appointed to the trusted powerful post of constable of Stirling Castle in 1368, while during the reign from 1390 to 1406, another Forsyth is recorded as being in receipt of a royal pension.

For several centuries afterwards, Forsyths continued to serve not only successive monarchs, but dominated the local affairs of Stirling and the surrounding area.

A William Forsyth, whose father was a baillie (civic official) in Edinburgh, in the mid to late fourteenth century, settled further north, at St Andrews, in 1423 – and it was here that he obtained the lucrative barony of Nydie.

Alexander Forsyth, 4th Baron of Nydie, and the sheriff depute of Fife, was among the 5,000 Scots including James IV, an archbishop, two bishops, eleven earls, fifteen barons, and 300 knights who were killed at the disastrous battle of Flodden in September of 1513.

The Scottish monarch had embarked on the venture after Queen Anne of France, under the terms of the Auld Alliance between Scotland and her nation, appealed to him to 'break a lance' on her behalf and act as her chosen knight.

Crossing the border into England at the head of a 25,000-strong army that included 7,500 clansmen and their kinsmen, James engaged a 20,000-strong force commanded by the Earl of Surrey.

Despite their numerical superiority and bravery, however, the Scots proved no match for the skilled English artillery and superior military tactics of Surrey.

Descendants of the baron of Nydie who fell at Flodden later acquired lands near the magnificent Falkland Palace, where they served as favoured royal courtiers – and the chief of today's Clan Forsyth traces his descent from this family.

In 1978 the Lord Lyon King of Arms of

Scotland, the recognised expert on matters of genealogy and heraldry, recognised Clan Forsyth, whose crest is a griffin and whose motto is 'A repairer of ruin', as one of the oldest in Scotland.

Forsyths have been prominent in the annals of Scotland's often turbulent religious history, not least a family of Forsyths from Annandale, in Dumfriesshire, who became Covenanting martyrs.

Described as 'the glorious marriage day of the kingdom with God', the National Covenant renounced Catholic belief, pledged to uphold the Presbyterian religion, and called for free parliaments and assemblies.

Signed at Edinburgh's Greyfriars Church on February 28, 1638 by Scotland's nobles, barons, burgesses and ministers, it was subscribed to the following day by hundreds of ordinary people, while copies were made and dispatched around Scotland and signed by thousands more.

Those who adhered to the Covenant were known as Covenanters, and many of them, hounded by the merciless authorities, literally took to the hills and valleys of Lowland Scotland to worship at what were known as open-air conventicles.

They were brutally suppressed, particularly after they rose in an armed revolt in 1679, achieving victory over government troops at the battle of Drumclog, near the Ayrshire village of Darvel on June 1 of that year.

Defeat followed only a few weeks later, however, at the battle of Bothwell Brig, in Lanarkshire.

Many Covenanters who were taken after battle or captured after being hunted down in the hills and valleys were summarily executed on the spot, while others had to endure harsh imprisonment.

In May of 1685, during the bloody period known as the Killing Time, James Forsyth was among 167 captured Covenanters, including five women, who were incarcerated in the forbidding fortress of Dunnottar Castle, south of Stonehaven, on the Kincardineshire coast.

Thrown into a dark, cramped, and fetid cellar with only two windows, the prisoners slowly succumbed to disease and starvation.

A number were removed to a dungeon beneath the cellar, where conditions were even worse.

This prompted the heartbroken wives of two of the prisoners to complain to the authorities of how '...they are not only in a starving condition but must inevitably incur a plague or other fearful diseases.'

No sympathy was forthcoming, however, and matters took a particularly brutal turn when James Forsyth's pregnant wife made the long journey on foot from Annandale to Dunnottar to visit her husband.

The castle governor promptly threw her into the dungeon, and left her to die in misery.

Tried beyond all endurance, twenty-five desperate prisoners managed to escape through one of the cellar's tiny windows and attempted a perilous descent down the steep cliffs on which the castle perched.

Two of them fell to their deaths while seven other prisoners died because of their brutal treatment.

A noted family of Forsyths was also settled at Monymusk, in Aberdeenshire, and their most famous son was the Reverend Alexander Forsyth, who was a Presbyterian minister at Belhelvie.

Born in 1769, Forsyth appears to have retained a vestige of the family's martial tradition in his genes, because when not preaching he was not only a keen game shooter, but immersed himself in the study of firearms.

He literally changed the face of modern warfare in 1807 when he invented the percussion cap, which gradually replaced the inefficient and outmoded flintlock.

The French Emperor Napoleon Bonaparte was quick to recognise the vital importance of the invention and offered Forsyth what was then the truly staggering sum of £20,000 for its secrets.

The patriotic inventor, however, turned down the offer.

But his patriotism appears to have been misplaced because his own government adopted the invention without his knowledge and only much later granted him a rather meagre pension – the first instalment of which was received on the day he died in 1848!

Aberdeenshire was also the birthplace of Peter Taylor Forsyth, better known as the influential theologian P.T. Forsyth.

Born in 1842, he studied at both the universities of Aberdeen and Gottingen, in Germany, before being ordained into the Congregationalist Church and later receiving the prestigious appointment of principal of Hackney Theological College, in London.

Chapter four:

World renown

While the Reverend Alexander Forsyth displayed a knack for invention, yet another Aberdeenshire Forsyth displayed creative talents, although of a rather more peaceful nature.

Born at Old Meldrum in 1737, William Forsyth was the distinguished horticulturist after whom the popular genus of plants known as *Forsythia* is named.

Studying for a number of years at the botanical gardens in Chelsea, the green-fingered Forsyth was appointed chief superintendent of the magnificent royal gardens at Kensington and St James's Palace in 1784.

A skilled researcher in all matters relating to plants, particularly those of diseases, it was Forsyth who discovered a particular composition, or mixture, which prevented diseases then common to fruit trees.

He became a best-selling author in 1802

with the publication of his *Treatise on the Culture and Management of Fruit Trees*, with all three editions selling out.

He died in 1804, in the rather apt setting of the horticultural grandeur of Kensington Gardens.

On the battlefield, Colonel James Forsyth is infamously remembered as the commander of the 7th U.S. Cavalry, responsible for the massacre of Lakota Indians at Wounded Knee in December of 1890.

More honourably, Samuel Forsyth, born in New Zealand in 1891, won the coveted Victoria Cross during the First World War for gallantry in an action at Grevillers, in France, in August of 1918.

Forsyth had led an attack on three German machine gun positions and taken their crews prisoner, but was later shot dead by a sniper while leading the crew of a disabled tank in another action.

In the world of sport, Tim Forsyth, born in 1973, is the retired Australian high jumper who won gold at the 1994 Commonwealth Games.

In the world of music Malcolm Forsyth, who was born in South Africa in 1936 but later immigrated to Canada, is the trombonist and composer who was named Canadian Composer of the Year in 1989 and who was made a member of the Order of Canada in 2003.

Recognised as one of the world's leading thriller writers, Frederick Forsyth is the novelist and political commentator who was born in Ashford, Kent, in 1938.

After studying at the University of Granada, in Spain, he joined the Royal Air Force, becoming, at the age of 19, one of its youngest pilots ever.

Leaving RAF service in 1958, he spent several years working as a newspaper reporter, before joining the worldwide Reuters news service in 1961 and later the BBC as assistant diplomatic correspondent.

He reported on the harrowing war in Biafra in 1967, and later left the BBC following allegations that his reporting had been biased in favour of the Biafran cause.

Undaunted, he returned to Biafra as a freelance journalist, and this culminated in his 1969 factual book *The Biafra Story*.

Turning his talents to fiction, his first novel, *The Day of the Jackal*, was published in 1971: concerning a plot to assassinate French President Charles de Gaulle, it was also adapted for film.

A string of further best-selling novels have followed, including *The Odessa File*, *The Dogs of War*, *The Fourth Protocol*, *The Fist of God*, and *Avenger*.

Also in the world of fiction is the best selling Australian fantasy writer Kate Forsyth, born in Sydney in 1966 and best known for her *Witches of Eileanan* series and the *Rhiannon's Ride* series.

Two leading figures in the world of contemporary entertainment are the London-born entertainer and showman Bruce Forsyth and the Glasgow-born film director and writer Bill Forsyth.

Bruce Forsyth, born in north London in

1928 as Bruce Forsyth-Johnson, first achieved fame in the British television show *Sunday Night at the London Palladium*, which ran from 1958 to 1961, and has subsequently presented a number of hugely popular television game shows in addition to co-hosting the *Strictly Come Dancing* series.

Bill Forsyth, born in 1946, is best known for his 1981 film *Gregory's Girl*, which won Best Screenplay in the 1981 BAFTA awards, the 1984 film *Comfort and Joy*, while he also wrote and directed *Local Hero*, starring Burt Lancaster.

Carrying on a Forsyth tradition of involvement in political affairs, baron Forsyth of Drumlean, is best known as the former British Conservative politician Michael Forsyth, who was born in Stirling in 1954.

He first entered parliament in the 1983 General Election, later serving for a time as Secretary of State for Scotland, but he lost his seat in the 1997 election.

A member of the House of Lords, he was also until July of 2005 deputy chairman of the J.P. Morgan investment bank, in London.

On a geographical note, 'Forsyth' is also the place name of at least four towns in the U.S.A. – in Georgia, Illinois, Missourri, and Montana.

It is also the proud name of several American counties, including Forsyth County in Georgia and Forsyth County in North Dakota.